SECRET OF LOST MOUNTAIN

AN ILLUSTRATED NOVEL

INSTRUCTOR'S MANUAL

BY

ARLENE SCOTT, M.A.

LOGOS INSTITUTE PRESS

Secret of Lost Mountain was written by
Bernard Scott
Illustrated by
Ronaldo Florendo

ISBN 978-0-9801174-5-5
(paperback)

Published by Logos Institute Press

http://logosinstitute.org

TABLE OF CONTENTS

ILLUSTRATIONS

i

PREFACE

This Instructor's Manual is designed to accompany the novel *Secret of Lost Mountain* by Bernard Scott, a short adventure novel that will appeal to young adults in Catholic settings. The manual is intended to help instructors guide young readers to gain an understanding of the elements of good fiction in general, and to stimulate thinking about the deeper themes and ideas presented in this particular novel.

Teachers, homeschooling parents, and group discussion leaders should find the questions and responses helpful in directing students to look beyond the story to such elements of good fiction as the development of plot with its rising action, climax, falling action and resolution; the point of view expressed in the novel and how this is accomplished; character and the manner in which character is transformed; the inclusion and significance of symbols; and, finally, the possible allegorical aspects of the story.

Each of these literary aspects is introduced with a brief explanation, followed by three sets of questions relating the literary aspects to this novel. These questions are graded for difficulty in order to accommodate students of different ages and capabilities. Questions labeled (A) are the least difficult; those designated (B) require a more complex analysis; and (C) are the most challenging. Although the questions are designed to stimulate group discussion, they can just as easily be transposed into writing assignments or examination questions.

Before presenting questions, it is recommended that the novel first be read in its entirety, since it has elements of mystery and secrecy that should be allowed to unfold as the plot unfolds. Afterward, the questions can be presented without becoming a plot spoiler. Students may, however, need some minimal guidance through the opening chapters to assure that they are comfortable with the complexity of the family history as presented and with the introduction of the primitive language, *Chiroki*.

SECRET OF LOST MOUNTAIN

BRIEF SYNOPSIS

An agnostic scientist turned explorer travels to a remote land to chase down rumors of a primitive tribe said to be wrapped in silence, silent even when they speak. How can this be? His pursuit for answers takes him up a dangerous river and ultimately to Lost Mountain. There he learns the awful secret that isolates this tribe. When the explorer finds more than he is questing for, the story takes on far deeper significance. Setting his scientific interests aside, he seeks a way to alleviate their plight. In the end, a series of mysterious events takes matters out of his hands, teaching him something far beyond the realm of natural science.

At the beginning of the novel, the reader notes that this scientist exhibits no interest whatsoever in things spiritual. But as the story develops, this man of science is taken, almost against his will, deeply into the very heart of religious deeds and beliefs, all of a most pronounced Catholic kind.

In what follows we include two of the ten illustrations provided for the novel by the illustrator Ronaldo Florendo.

The explorer arrives at the coastal port of a remote, far-off land.

SECRET OF LOST MOUNTAIN

DETAILED SYNOPSIS OF THE NOVEL

BY BERNARD SCOTT

An adventurous man of science (with a keen interest in obscure languages) comes across a dusty old manuscript in the library stacks at his university. The manuscript had been written many years earlier by a missionary priest (Fr. Christopher Damian, S.J.) while on mission in a remote, primitive part of the world. The manuscript tells of rumors of a strange people dwelling on a mountain deep in the interior of that country, a people, it was said, who make no sound when they speak, who live wrapped in total silence. The missionary wrote that he intended to go to them as a priest. but the manuscript does not reveal whether, in fact, he ever did. The man of science in this story is wholly taken with the priest's account of a far-off people who make no noise of any kind, not even when they go about their daily lives, and he decides to explore the mystery himself.

This is where the story opens. This protagonist, as an explorer now, has just arrived at the coastland of this remote land with plans to go into the interior and find this fabled mountain tribe. Coastlanders warn him he will have to navigate the great river past hostile river tribes, any of whom would think nothing of killing him. Other coastlanders merely laugh and wonder how he could believe such rumors. However, on the coastland the explorer encounters a lone member of the aborigine tribe, the *Chiroki*, who live by the headwaters of the great river, near this mystery mountain. His name is *Teeku* and he confirms the truth of this strange rumor.

From this aborigine, the explorer learns some stunning things about this mystery tribe. No one has ever seen them but, yes, they are there on that mountain and they are silent. They are silent because they are deaf, and not only deaf, they are also blind. How this could be, how deaf-blind people could ever survive on their own is one of the mysteries the explorer intends to unravel.

Teeku also tells him of the priest who had come to the *Chiroki* years ago. It seemed to the *Chiroki* that this priest displayed healing powers and, as a result, they sought to bring him to Lost Mountain to heal the deaf-blind there. But the priest never fulfilled this mission. On his way to Lost Mountain, he was attacked by an animal and almost killed. *Teeku* was selected by the *Chiroki* chief to bring the priest down river to the coast for medical help, and he did so, but the priest was beyond help. Before he died, the priest made *Teeku* promise to return to his people with a magical amulet (called *Odilia sannu* in the *Chiroki* language) which the priest had worn around his neck. *Teeku* was to give it to the *Chiroki* chief, along with a strange, single-sentence message saying the priest offers his "death" for "them." This merely increases the puzzle and the explorer's determination to uncover the mystery of this deaf-blind tribe.

The great river he must travel up is dangerous but the explorer is not afraid, and with *Teeku's* help, he prepares for the journey. He purchases a gun and outfits a sturdy canoe. From *Teeku* he learns to say simple things in the *Chiroki* language. As the day of departure arrives, *Teeku* hands the explorer the amulet (in actuality a saint's relic) that had been worn by the priest and that *Teeku* had promised to convey to the *Chiroki* chief. Now *Teeku* asks the explorer to fulfill that promise. As it turns out, this *Odilia sannu* lies behind a string of unusual events as the explorer unwittingly retraces the priest's steps in more ways than he ever foresaw.

The river journey is punctuated with drama of its own, but at its end the explorer reaches the village of the *Chiroki* tribe and is brought before the *Chiroki* chief, the *Sabuknu*. Initially things do not go well. However, when the *Chiroki* see the explorer wearing the magic relic, they take him for another priest and begin to venerate him. As a man of science and modern-day agnostic, the explorer is uncomfortable with his new persona, but because they see him as a healer, they readily concede to his wish to go to Lost Mountain, and the son of the *Chiroki* chief, *Teeku-mi*, is picked to lead him there. This native prince reveals that these deaf-blind people were also once *Chiroki* who, due to an ancient curse, were banished as babies to Lost Mountain, chiefly to placate the evil spirits there responsible for cursing the *Chiroki* with this terrible affliction. The outcasts are called *Jakareme*, children of the curse, and they are believed to have survived on the mountain in some

4

mysterious, fearful manner. *Teeku-mi* tells the explorer that he had a daughter named Sweet Berry who was born deaf and blind and who, in accordance with tribal custom, was automatically banished as a *Jakareme* to Lost Mountain. No one can be sure she is still alive, but the native prince is openly expecting the explorer-priest will find his daughter and heal her. Because of the native's very real fear of evil spirits, *Teeku-mi* takes the explorer only up to the drop-off on Lost Mountain, the site where the babies like his daughter are left to the evil mountain spirits. It is agreed that in nine days the native prince will return and lead the explorer back down the mountain. But of course the native prince is expecting that on his return he will find his daughter healed. To the agnostic explorer, just as surely, this expectation is a most troublesome impossibility that he will have to deal with later.

On his own now on Lost Mountain, the explorer discovers a vine trail and follows it to a settlement of crude bamboo huts all carefully linked by vine lines. These huts house the *Jakareme*, the name of these deaf-blind people, the so-called "children (*reme*) of the curse" (*jaka*). There are about seventy of them, of all ages, ruled by their own aged, deaf-blind chief. Unbeknown to them, the explorer initially mingles among these *Jakareme* and studies their ways, their hand signs, their methods of gathering and preparing food, making clothes, and so on. When one of the *Jakareme* teenagers falls and breaks an arm, the explorer sets the bone, and in the process he gives his presence away. Through a series of events, their initial fear and hostility to this unseen, inexplicably different intruder in their midst eventually gives way to cautious acceptance, in no small measure because of his decision to act like a *Jakareme* himself, as one like them. The *Jakareme* of course sense he is different in some way, but they have no inkling of its extent, of what it would mean for someone to see and hear.

The explorer discovers a cave nearby that begins to unravel the mystery of how abandoned babies could ever have survived on Lost Mountain let alone organize a reasonably well-functioning settlement. In this cave he finds a lovely *Chiroki* woman who both sees and hears him. It turns out that she is the rejected wife of the *Chiroki* chief's son, the native prince who brought the explorer-priest to the mountain. So she is the mother of their daughter Sweet Berry, the little deaf-blind girl the explorer is supposed to heal. Unknown to the *Chiroki*, this woman had followed her daughter to Lost Mountain.

The explorer realizes that other mothers of cursed children had done the same, over many generations. It was these mothers of the deaf-blind, themselves considered cursed, who kept the infants alive and, over generations, gradually formed the *Jakareme's* living arrangements.

The woman in the cave is weak with malaria, and the explorer administers drugs and brings her back to health. In the process, he becomes attracted to her. She takes him for a priest and, seeing that he carries the legendary magic object, *Odilia sannu,* she too expects him to cure her daughter Sweet Berry.

As per their arrangement, the *Chiroki* prince, *Teeku-mi*, arrives at the original spot on Lost Mountain where nine days before he had left the pseudo priest. Now the explorer is faced with grave difficulties. He must first convince this native that the evil mountain spirits have been banished and that their curse on the tribe has been lifted. He must then get the prince to follow him to the settlement, and then to the cave where his estranged wife and also Sweet Berry will be waiting. At this point, the native prince still does not know if his daughter Sweet Berry has been healed. Nor, in fact, does the explorer, although a strange happening involving *Odilia sannu* leads him (and the reader of the novel) to wonder that perhaps a miracle of healing might indeed have occurred. But it is unclear at this stage of the tale and the truth of the matter is not established until the native prince himself enters the cave, encounters his long lost wife, and lays eyes on his daughter. The reader is not privy to this encounter. All the reader knows is that *Teeku-mi* rushes out of the cave and falls prostrate at the feet of the explorer.

This story is told in three distinct narrative accounts. The first is entitled "The Father's Tale." This presents the story of Lost Mountain as a father's bedtime entertainment to his daughter, Daisy. The second is entitled "The Explorer's Account," and consists of the explorer's own running record of his adventures on Lost Mountain, dictated real time into a voice recorder. The third and final account is "Daisy's Epilogue" which completes the story left unfinished by her father. In the end, we learn some rather surprising things concerning *Odilia sannu* whose relic caused so many mysterious things to happen in this novel. The disclosures might cause some readers to wonder where the line between fiction and reality is to be drawn.

The explorer encounters his first *Jakareme* on Lost Mountain

SECRET OF LOST MOUNTAIN

LITERARY ANALYSIS

BY ARLENE SCOTT

The story line of *Secret of Lost Mountain* has enough adventure, intrigue, and unfolding secrets to keep most readers turning the pages. However, beyond the novel's fascinating story line, a certain literary richness also unfolds.

The novel can be read at several levels: an adventure story; an allegory about life; a conversion story; a quest that results in transformation. As an adventure story, *Secret of Lost Mountain* is filled with suspense over a number of events, moving the reader to read for outcomes. It is set amid difficult physical circumstances and has abundant forward movement: the explorer's physical journey up the river, his dramatic encounter with the *Chiroki* tribe, and then his remarkable experiences with the *Jakareme* on Lost Mountain.

As an allegory, the novel is a tale that suggests more than it says—the external events serve as vehicle for a deeper understanding of human frailty and its healing, not only as it relates to the *Chiroki* and to the poor, benighted *Jakareme*, but, ironically, even more as it relates to the explorer himself.

The story also touches on the prejudices and negative attitudes that not only the *Chiroki* but almost everyone holds toward people who are significantly different from them, people they don't understand. The *Chiroki* reject the weakest and most vulnerable in their community. They too have pondered the same question that was asked of Christ: *"Rabbi, was it his sin or that of his parents that caused him to be born blind?"* (John 9:2), and for their part they lay the blame on an ancient, ancestral murder, much like that of Cain in the *Genesis* story. To this agnostic explorer, of course, there is only a modern scientific answer to that question, one having to do with disordered genes.

As a conversion story, or a story of transformation, the reader notes the irony that the explorer, this "son of the enlightenment," is himself "blind" to spiritual realities. In his pursuit of a curious phenomenon in the interest of science, the explorer finds more than he sought—a new-found encounter with healing power beyond anything science can explain. The explorer is moved by the condition of the *Jakareme* to set aside his scientific purposes in order to help them, as one human being to another. The acts of the explorer begin to mirror those of the original priest whose writings had so intrigued him in the first place. In the end, despite himself, the explorer becomes the essence of a priest—someone who offers sacrifice for the benefit of others, in this case himself.

Religious belief—and unbelief—play a key role, therefore, in this story. The agnostic explorer, the man of science, finds himself being drawn into a faith system based on the most unlikely of evidence: inexplicable events associated with a relic or, as he calls it, "the bone chip of a saint." He discovers that the *Chiroki* believe the relic he wore has miraculous powers to heal in ways unthinkable to a modern scientist. But by the story's end, this skeptical man of science had no choice to but to believe in that power himself.

In another respect the story describes the meeting between modern civilization and primitive life. The irony is that modern civilization has lost any sense of faith, whereas the primitives are ridden with belief in the preternatural, both good and bad. Correctly, in a way, the explorer, who represents modern civilization, sees through the primitives' superstitions and strives to dispel their fears of evil spirits on Lost Mountain. He attempts to do this from his standpoint of scientific rationality.

Ironically, what ultimately succeeds in dispelling the primitives' fear of these dark forces is not reason but the relic of a forgotten faith, forgotten as far as modern civilization is concerned. It is the relic (the power that underlies it) that not only frees these primitives of dark superstitions, but also changes the heart of this man of science himself.

Secret of Lost Mountain thus can be seen as a transformation story. By the story's end, the man of science finds himself doing a lot more than gathering data for scientific purposes. Despite himself, this erzatz priest follows in the footsteps of a real priest, and in a way in Christ's footsteps as well, becoming a kind of unconscious Christ-like figure, going about doing good among the unfortunate *Jakareme*, healing the afflicted and feeding the hungry. As we see, the explorer's own identity undergoes progressive metamorphoses: from professor to explorer to pseudo "priest," even to a medical doctor like his own father, and then to a *Jakareme*. And finally, for a transformative moment, it appears he turns into the real priest, Christopher Damian. As a consequence of the miracles that *Odilia sanna* works through him, he transforms the *Jakareme* into *Odiliareme*, reconciling them with the *Chiroki*. And the personal lives of the native prince *Teeku-mi,* his wife *Tolani*, and their child Sweet Berry will also be transformed.

Other themes run through the story as well. For example, language plays a huge role in the novel. Certain reflective passages about language might stimulate philosophical thought in some readers about how language affects our perception of our world and forms our culture.

Another major theme deals with family relationships. The novel offers many reflections on the meaning of fatherhood and motherhood, all stimulated by what the explorer finds and does not find among these primitives. Ironically, this man of science, estranged from his own wife and son, is profoundly affected by the familial relationships he discovers among the *Jakareme,* where he sees father-son relationships formed among those who are not blood-related. So here we have a case of the primitive world restoring a kind of spiritual health to a civilized man who had lost any relationship with his own son, but who now leaves his experience of the primitive world resolved to restore it.

And finally, the explorer leaves the primitive world with an understanding and appreciation of the cryptic words written by the first priest, Fr. Christopher Damian, addressed to *Teeku*: *"Tell Sabuknu I offer my death for them."* As we learn, like the original priest that he has unwittingly come to imitate, the explorer fulfills that message with his own death.

It could be said that *Secret of Lost Mountain* is essentially a Christian story, even a quintessentially Catholic story, with its references to priesthood, saints, relics, and miraculous healings. The belief that "the bone chip of a saint" should be reverenced and that, in praying to saints, a miraculous result can be effected is a particularly Catholic view. However, one need not ascribe to Catholic belief in order to be moved by the plight of the *Jakareme* and to delight in their eventual redemption through the ministrations of an agnostic explorer who ultimately is turned into a "priest."

Putting it into the broader religious concept, *Secret of Lost Mountain* is a salvation story. The final pages of the story recall the words of Jesus that *"There is no greater love than this; to lay down one's life for one's friends"* (John 15:13). The explorer no sooner encounters the *Jakareme* than he "lays down" his scientific focus and takes up a work of love for these disadvantaged people. In the end, a real priest and an erzatz "priest" both give their lives to effect a new and better life for a group of most unfortunate outcasts.

LITERARY TOPICS FOR DISCUSSION OR ESSAY WITH SUGGESTED RESPONSES AND OBSERVATIONS

PLOT

In novels, dramas, and short stories, the plot is traditionally structured around the following elements:

Exposition: The exposition offers background to the situation of the story by setting the scene and offering the reader necessary background about the main character (the protagonist) and delineating what type of antagonist he faces Often, in a novel, background exposition is supplied piecemeal as events develop, or may be provided through flashbacks.

Rising action: The rising action originates at that moment in the exposition when the protagonist encounters a conflict or crisis of some kind. The conflict may be either internal (the protagonist must resolve it by dealing with some crisis within) or external, in which case the protagonist is pitted against antagonistic forces outside him/herself, such as another character, society, or nature. Not infrequently, both internal and external factors are involved.

And often, the protagonist encounters not just one crisis, but a series of crises, each of them intensifying suspense or tension until the story reaches its climax.

Climax: The climax of a work of fiction is the moment of highest tension in the story, that moment the reader has been anticipating throughout.

Falling action: This occurs after the climax, as outcomes are revealed and tension is relieved.

Resolution: Often referred to as the *denouement*, plot resolution consists of those final moments in the plot when all the key issues are disclosed and dealt with. (*Dénouement* is a French term which translates as "the untying of the knot.")

QUESTIONS ABOUT PLOT

A

▪ The explorer, the protagonist of *Secret of Lost Mountain,* is faced with a ***series of crises*** throughout the plot. What are some of the major crises the explorer must confront?

B

▪ What would you say is the ***climax***, the moment of highest tension in this novel?

▪ Are you satisfied with the ***resolution*** of that climax in the closing chapters of this novel?

▪ Are all the aspects of the various conflicts sufficiently unraveled, or are you left wishing for more explanation?

C

▪ Based on the outline of ***plot*** given above, can you identify the key moments and events of this novel that relate to these elements of plot (*exposition, rising action, etc.*)?

RESPONSES AND OBSERVATIONS ABOUT PLOT

A. Series of Crises

The explorer encounters numerous crises as he pursues his quest to find out about the tribe "wrapped in silence" on Lost Mountain.

- The trip up the river with its threats of hostile tribes.
- The confrontation on the river by the *Chiroki* tribe.
- The explorer's rejection by the *Sabuknu* (*Chiroki* tribal chief)
- Mistaken identity, being taken for a priest and expected to act like one.

- The burden placed on him by *Teeku-mi*, who expects the explorer to work the healing of his daughter Sweet Berry.

- Finding a way into the *Jakareme* community without alienating them and their chief.

- Figuring out how to get the *Chiroki* to give up their superstitious rejection of the *Jakareme* and receive them back into the tribe.

- The healing of Sweet Berry.

B. Climax and Resolution

The answer to the question of climax may be left open to discussion, but most readers will likely agree that they were hoping to learn if the relic would actually return sight to Sweet Berry. Interestingly, the climatic moments of the novel are now no longer described in the explorer's own words. His batteries have died out and what we learn from that point on is only through second-hand accounts, supposedly derived from the explorer's notes as he journeyed back down the great river. This once-removed description of the novel's climax is intentional on the part of the author, and makes for interesting literary technique.

- The author does not describe exactly what happens when the explorer, beside himself, applies the relic to her eyes. The reader is purposely kept in suspense.

- Later when the light from his flashlight disturbs the sleep of Sweet Berry, we can suspect that her reaction occurred because she can now see. But neither the reader nor the explorer can be sure.

- It is only near the end, with *Teeku-mi's* deep bow of gratitude before the explorer/priest, that we understand the miracle has truly occurred. Everything we want to know is encapsulated in that prostration, making it the moment of the novel's deepest climax.

The resolution of all the loose ends is recounted by Daisy who in turn is merely reporting what her father gleaned from the explorer's notes. We are told that traders obtained these notes from the river tribes. How they fell into the father's hands is not explained. Moreover, the precise fate of the explorer is not ours to know but we are given to believe that he was killed on the river by hostile tribes. This final resolution is only speculation, but the reader is given to believe it the most likely one.

- Although we may wish for more certitude about these issues, we cannot place blame on the author for a somewhat hazy resolution of these matters. After all, we willingly placed ourselves in the hands of Daisy, who placed herself in the hands of her father, who based his knowledge on recovered tapes and documents, and, more than likely, his own rich imagination.

- In a way it is the very uncertainty of the explorer's final fate that allows the story to tug at the reader's heart and mind, for it leaves the reader with much to think and wonder about. As the subtitle claims: *Secret of Lost Mountain* is "a story for youthful imaginations of all ages."

C. Plot Structure of the Novel

Exposition:

- Original reason for the adventure.

- Arrival at the coastland; skepticism of the coastlanders.

- Background regarding the priest Christopher Damian, S.J.

- Learning from *Teeku* about the people on Lost Mountain.

- Information about the great river and its dangers.

Rising Action and Series of Crises:

- Confrontation with river tribes and with a *Chiroki* armada.

- Rejection by the *Chiroki* chief, the *Sabuknu.*

- A difficult night in the rain storm.

- Being mistaken for a priest and expected to act like one.

- Finding a way to work his way into the *Jakareme* community.

- Bringing *Tolani* into his plan.

Climax:

- Apparent healing of Sweet Berry in the cave.

- *Teeky-mi* falling prostrate at the explorer's feet near the end of the tale, confirming the miracle.

Falling Action:

- The explorer's trip down the mountain and the veneration shown him by the two accompanying native warriors.

- The explorer's final, dramatic deed back in the *Chiroki* village (see **Resolution**, below).

- The journey on the great river to return home, a journey never completed as far as any of the narrators know.

Resolution:

- Burning of the purple sashes of *all* Chiroki women who bore deaf-blind children, signifying the restoration of the *Jakareme* to their *Chiroki* kinsmen as full members of the tribe.

- The burning of the sashes also signifies to the *Chiroki* that the evil spirits have been banished from Lost Mountain. Now the mountain is no longer "lost" to them.

POINT OF VIEW

In fiction, the point of view of the storyteller is critical in shaping the way the reader receives the story. The point of view of a piece of fiction is not necessarily the author's point of view and readers should not confuse the author with the person to whom the author entrusts the telling of his story. Such a narrator may tell us as much or as little as he chooses; he may interpret the activities and thoughts of the characters for us, or he may leave us guessing what the characters' reactions are so that we have to figure things out for ourselves.

Some stories have omniscient narrators who can tell us what is in the minds of all the characters and can also interpret why they act as they do. Some stories have narrators with limited omniscience. The narrator could perhaps be one of the characters in the story who is as limited as the reader in knowing why the other characters act and speak as they do.

Some stories have reliable narrators and other have unreliable narrators. In this particular novel, the story is told by three different narrators: the father, Daisy, and the explorer. The father and Daisy are somewhat unreliable as narrators in that both stand outside the story itself, and they are recounting a tale that may or may not be true. Daisy tells us it was never clear to her how much of the story was true and how much was made up. However, when the story's narration comes directly from the explorer, who stands within the story, and who relates events into his tape recorder as they occur, the reader gains confidence that a reliable narrator has entered the scene and we tend more readily to suspend disbelief and accept all that he tells us.

QUESTIONS ABOUT POINT OF VIEW

A

- What are the early *truth claims* by Daisy and her father, and also by the coastlanders, that tend to convince the reader this is a tale of pure fantasy?

- How do these same narrators at other times suggest, to the contrary, that the story may actually have occurred?

B

- As a **reliable narrator**, how does the explorer's account create a sense of reality and credibility about this community of deaf-blind people and the events of the story?

- When the explorer's batteries run out, what is the effect of losing the first-person, reliable narrator just as the climax of the story occurs? Does it weaken or actually heighten the sense of reality?

C

- What is the impact of having **three narrators**, the father, the explorer, and finally Daisy? Does the switching back and forth between these narrators strengthen or weaken the sense that these events might have actually occurred? Did the lack of absolute clarity about the story's climax [the curing of Sweet Berry's blindness] weaken or strengthen the emotional impact on you, the reader?

RESPONSES AND OBSERVATIONS ABOUT POINT OF VIEW

A (1). Claims the Story is Purely Fiction:

- The book's subtitle claims that it is "*a tale for youthful imaginations of all ages.*"

- Daisy asked her father to tell her a story about "*a place no one would suspect could even exist.*" (1)

- Daisy adds: "*How much of this story might actually be true and how much of it is just made up I do not really know.*" (1)

- Her father's narrative begins: "*Imagine a strange world hidden back in the remotest mountains of a poor, distant land, a secret place with inhabitants so unusual in fact that, had word of it ever reached the civilized world, people would have scoffed. And, indeed, no one in the civilized world had the faintest notion such a thing could actually be.*" (2)

- The father adds: *"No coastlander had ever seen these people."* (2)

- The coastlanders who live near the mountain attest that *"that part of the mountains cannot be entered. . . . Who knows what might be up there?"* (2)

- *"If you asked the coastlanders about it, the more educated simply shook their head and laughed at the notion."* (2)

- *"When asked if the stories were true that there existed a mountain tribe [that] lives in complete silence, [and that] makes no noise nor sound of any kind, not even when they speak,"* the narrator tells us that *"the port official smirked and said nothing. . . . As far as this official was concerned, this story was unworthy of comment."* (4)

A (2). Claims the Story May Be Real:

- Daisy states in her opening: *"Perhaps you will receive this story in much the same way that I did, as something compelling with its own kind of beauty."* Daisy adds: *"I feel it must be shared before it is lost to time."* (1)

- *"My father told me of a people and of a circumstance so strange and yet so real I still feel their presence near me today."* (1)

- *"But the poor and unschooled had little doubt about it."* (2)

- The scientist/explorer claims to have read about the silent tribe in his native country.

- The explorer had received this information from a reliable source, a Jesuit priest who was a scholar.

- When the explorer meets *Teeku*, the native confirms the rumors and explains the mystery of their silence: the people are deaf-blind!

- The truth of their plight seems believable because the priest had actually intended to go to them and heal them.

- Carlito's father produces a manila envelope with further documentation discovered to be in the handwriting of the same priest.

B. Reliable Narrator

- The reader is likely to accept more readily this rather incredible story when the explorer begins describing what he finds into his tape recorder. After all, he is a scientist so we expect objective information from him together with credible explanations. And that's what we get. He is a first person, reliable narrator who convinces us of the credibility of such a community of deaf-blind living together.

- After the explorer's batteries die out, the switch back to the less reliable narrator was intended to add credibility to the explorer's first-person account, as if now we are being given an independent witness as to its actuality. Claims about recovered documents, etc., were meant to strengthen the impression that the events of the story might really have happened.

- According to the author, one of his purposes was to make the line between reality and fiction seem uncertain, i.e., to leave the reader wondering whether something so fanciful as this might not have a basis in reality. The author's intent of course is not to deceive but to create wonder, one of the objectives of good imaginative writing, in this case wonder as to whether any of this could in some way actually be true. Of course we know it isn't but the pleasure lies in thinking it just might be so.

C. Impact of Three Narrators

- There is a calculated haziness at the outset about whether we're being told something that actually happened or something fabricated. The reader is at a third remove from the action: the narrator (Daisy) is telling a story that someone (her father) had told her. Her father had learned the details from old documents that supposedly were real. The narrators, however, are all in agreement as to what happened, which would seem to encourage suspension of disbelief.

- Once again, at the story's end, the haziness returns. The explorer's batteries run out, and the reliable narrator is again replaced by an unreliable one, Daisy. We are forced to observe the denouement through the mist of someone's reported memories. *Secret of Lost Mountain* seems like an instance of *Brigadoon*— and for a moment the reader may enjoy the thought that these things really happened. At least that is the intent of good fiction.

- The haze gets even thicker as Daisy tells us that no one knows what exactly happened to the explorer, yet despite this, the emotional impact of what has happened may not allow the reader to immediately dismiss these events as obviously made-up.

- Like the jolt of an electric shock, the distance between fantasy and reality tends to shrink when, in the *Afterword*, the author informs us that Odilia is in fact a real person, a bona fide saint. And moreover, like Sweet Berry, she was blind. This historical Odilia was also rejected by her father just as was Sweet Berry, and also because of it, curiously, she too spent time in a cave, and in the end she too is reconciled with her father. (It may be interesting to note that the author says none of this was known to him when he began the story.)

CHARACTER

The central character in a work of fiction (the protagonist) finds him/herself in a conflict with an antagonist of some sort. The antagonist may be the setting itself, like a dangerous sea voyage, or a searing desert heat. Or it may be another character who opposes, resists, or eludes the protagonist, Or the antagonist could be a set of circumstances unfriendly to the protagonist (a job loss, rejection by others, etc.). In many instances, the antagonist lies *within* the character himself or herself, (a flaw of temperament, an emotional reaction). Often as not, it is is some combination of these things.

Characters in fiction are often labeled as flat or round. A flat character is one-dimensional, having limited qualities by which to be judged. Round characters are complex, emotionally, intellectually, morally. In *Secret of Lost Mountain*, we are concerned with the explorer's quest as a scientist to discover the "secret" of Lost Mountain. Strangely, even though the explorer is a "round" character, the author does not give him a name, though everyone else in the story has one. We do not even know the country or language of his origin. He is a sort of representative person—a professor, a linguist, a scientist, a son of the Enlightenment, an agnostic, an explorer—an anyone or an everyman. This appears to be a purposeful omission by the author, leaving room in order to allow for his continued identity changes. (See question B below).

Fictional characters who are *static* remain unchanged throughout the work. *Dynamic* characters undergo personal transformation that is made to appear credible as they contend with the challenges presented in the plot. In this novel, the explorer is a good example of this. He is a complex person who in the course of the story gradually undergoes transformation. For example, the family relationships he witnesses among the primitives causes much self-reflection and desire for change in his own family life, particularly with his son; his encounter with religious faith affects his agnostic views; and his encounter with the needs of the *Jakareme* transforms his desire merely to study them for the purpose of science. If the author has portrayed the explorer as a credible character, the reader will believe in the changes in the explorer's eventual transformation at the end.

QUESTIONS ABOUT CHARACTER

A

- The protagonist undergoes *identity changes* many times throughout the novel. What are some of these identity changes?

B

- In the depiction of the explorer, where do you see a *conflict* between the original scientist and the emerging humanitarian? Between the agnostic and the man of faith?

C

- What would you consider the ultimate *transformation* of the protagonist?

RESPONSES AND COMMENTARY

A. Identity changes

- The explorer undergoes many identity changes:

  1) The original *professor* and man of science becomes

  2) an *explorer*, who then becomes

  3) a *priest* (pseudo-priest), then

  4) a *medical doctor*, like his father, who goes around dressing wounds and curing sickness. He then becomes

  5) an acting *Jakareme* who

  6) exchanges identity strings with *Sweet Berry*; and finally

  7) he becomes another *Fr. Christopher Damian* whose place the explorer seems actually to take for a brief moment of time near the story's end.

- At the story's end, as the price of helping the *Jakareme*, the explorer too must give up his life just as did Fr. Damian, the real priest, whose path the explorer unwittingly traces throughout this tale.

- Finally. we can detect at the tale's end another, subtler transformation as well, that of his self-understanding as a *father*, and his intention to mend his relationship with an estranged and long-neglected son.

- We see this already reflected in his concern for the welfare of Carlito, as evidenced by the explorer's plan at the story's end to give the young Carlito his canoe as a means of livelihood.

The explorer reflects on his own identity changes:

- He is mistaken for a priest by the *Chiroki*, and ponders that to them he must seem like *"someone who does unimaginable things. Oddly, that night on the altar mound flashed through [his] mind just then. That was unimaginable."* (94)

- *"If I am to enter into the life of this community, there is only one course to take: I have to become a* Jakareme.*"* (107)

- *"This is the second time* Odilia sannu *has changed my identity, just at the point where I needed to be seen in a new way entirely. First she made me a priest and now here I am a* Jakareme.*"* (109)

B. Conflicting Identities of the Explorer

The agnostic explorer's original, purely scientific intentions in this adventure evolve into a noble, humanitarian one; his original agnosticism is challenged by the inexplicable powers manifested through "the bone of a saint." To fulfill his seemingly preordained mission, the man of science must become what he is not: a kind of priest and, for a time, even a *Jakareme*. And at the end, though it is not stated so explicitly, the reader is led to believe that the explorer's agnosticism has given way to the beginnings of true faith.

At the outset, for the explorer, the people on the mountain are merely objects of scientific observation.

- *"All he wanted was to look around and gather what data he could about their number, the arrangement of their communal life, such as it was, and most importantly . . . how a band of deaf-blind like this managed to communicate with each other, and for that matter ever managed to hold onto life."* (66)

Due to mistaken identity engendered by the relic, the man of science finds himself in a fraudulent and untenable position as he is vested as priest and brought to an altar mound. But the experience begins to change him.

- *"And now, here he was . . . a man who had no religion, robed as a priest before an altar he would have to approach in very short order. What was he supposed to do?"* (70)

His first prayer arises within him, almost without his will:

- *"Looking up desperately at the night sky, moonless and dark, the false priest groaned inwardly for something, someone to wake him from this nightmare."* (71)

- *"He closed his eyes, lowered his head and whispered a plea, likely the first actual prayer that ever escaped his lips."* (72)

Something spiritual occurs within the man of science:

- *"Matters had changed. Inexplicably, whatever it was that took place on the altar mound just now was having its effect on everyone, including this explorer turned priest. And true enough, strange as it might seem to say this, the explorer too, from that moment on, found himself wishing that the miracle Teeku-mi was asking of him might truly take place on dundi kano. That something as far-fetched as this might really be so."* (73)

Nevertheless, the man of science is at war with the man of religious belief.

- *"The explorer was uneasy about something he wore as well, the saint's relic hanging down from his neck. He was no priest. Nothing of the sort. He only bore the relic because without it he would not be on his way to dundi lano. . . . As he and Teeku-mi set out, picking through the jungle brush, more than once he wanted to take the bothersome thing off and shove it in his backpack. But he found he couldn't remove it. Couldn't bring himself to do it. He didn't know why. Perhaps because it was now part of his identity, for the duration. And just possibly what had happened the other night on the altar mound had affected him in some way. He couldn't fathom it, frankly."* (75-76)

The concerned humanitarian gradually overcomes the objective scientist in the explorer's psyche. The explorer's scientific attitude tempers into one of compassion and humanity.

- *"I've developed an unaccountable urge to help these poor benighted souls, maybe every bit as much as Christopher Damian, strange as that is for me to say. And this crazy relic may be just the thing I need to make that happen. Oddly enough, that's something else I have in common with the priest."* (155)

- *"Why do I care? Why am I doing these things? I am hard put to say, and I confess it puzzles me not a little. I am a linguist and I came up to the* Jakareme *to satisfy a linguist's curiosity, nothing more, and now here I find myself putting aside my research, fretting instead about these poor people's welfare. It's as if some mysterious, hidden purpose has ruled this entire adventure from the start, in accord with some inexplicable inner logic of its own. The logic, whatever it is, mystifies me no end, but I can well imagine the good Reverend linguist Christopher Damian is enjoying a good chuckle over it. I have to laugh myself at what's happened. Perhaps I'm simply another of these little miracles* Odilia sannu *keeps springing on me."* (168)

- *"I see this business is getting to me too. With the little time I have left here I should be collecting data on their language, and here I am fixing roofs instead. Figure that one out."* (153)

C. The Protagonist's Ultimate Transformation

By the story's end, the happenings triggered by the saint's relic bring about a transformation in the agnostic man of science. But this happens very gradually.

Well into the story, though he wished that the miraculous healing of Sweet Berry might take place, he had no faith whatsoever that it could or would be so.

- *"Here's this fantasy of terror that has the* Chiroki *paralyzed, and here's this bone chip of a dead woman from halfway around the world about to liberate them. And all this because of an imposter priest who happens to scorn both the curse they fear and the miracle they dream of.*" (163)

- "*I could not lie to this woman, but I could answer what I truly believed, 'Odilia sannu would remove curse.'*" (162) Here, by removing the curse, the explorer meant only that the *Chiroki* would no longer see the *Jakareme* as cursed. He had no idea that blindness might be cured, none whatsoever at this point.

Sweet Berry has faith where he does not. She gets him to kiss the relic:

- "*. . . the little girl stretched out her hand . . . and feeling for my mouth, placed* Odilia *squarely on my lips. I too was to kiss* Odilia. *And in fact, with* Tolani *looking on, that's exactly what I did;* Katalan [*Chiroki* word for *priest*] *could hardly do otherwise.*" (175)

The explorer gradually comes to express faith in the mysterious powers associated with the relic, a faith even he can't rationalize:

- *But somehow I never seriously doubted this was going to turn out well. All because of this crazy relic of some unknown saint. When I thought of all the weird twists and turns that have taken place up to this point because of her, the uncanny way she has of making the most improbable things happen, I had no reason to doubt she would finish whatever it was she started. My place was simply to let this* Odilia *have her way. I have to admit I hardly recognized myself in these thoughts. How could a man of science and an avowed agnostic think this way? Good question. There I was, scientific work abandoned, scheming to help these poor, benighted souls, and banking on the bone of a long-dead woman to pull it off. What can I say? It's beyond explaining.*" (173)

Finally, in this man of science we see emerge actual, efficacious faith in the possibility of miracle:

- "*He held* Odilia *on each eye for a long time. He wanted to pray but he couldn't. But at that very moment the priest Damian came to mind and somehow, in his heart, this priest prayed the prayer he himself was incapable of. That this little girl would be healed. . . . And indeed there was prayer, long and ardent prayer, prayer with the faith of a real priest, a priest who offered his life for the well-being of these tragic souls, the Reverend Father Christopher Damian, S.J. Indeed, for a telling while the explorer seemed to become this priest, offering himself for this little girl and her loving mother. That God would perform a miracle. On his own, the explorer could never say he believed in any of this. But in that moment, outside himself, he believed in the priest Damian, and this priest believed in a miracle-working saint, and this saint believed in a God of miracles, a God who could do anything He wished. It's what makes a saint a saint and even an agnostic man of science had to acknowledge this. At a certain point in life, like at this moment, even he would trust that it must be so."* (188-189)

- *"The one-time priest in that moment knew the truth. In the shining, glistening eyes of the* Chiroki *prince he saw what he had not dared to see or even dared to hope for. But there it was, no mistaking. In that face, in its marvelous, glorious radiance, the explorer too saw the miracle."* (199)

Eventually, despite his initial unbelief, the man of science completes the mission for which he was sent: to effect a miraculous healing. The man of science, following in the footsteps of a martyred priest, also sacrificed his life for these lost *Jakareme* souls:

- *"Perhaps, like the Jesuit priest Christopher Damian whom he came to imitate despite himself, the explorer also wound up giving his life for these people."* (200)

- The cryptic message meant much to him now: "*Teeku*, Tell *Sabuknu* I offer my death for them." (201)

THEME

Just as in music where a theme is a recurring set of sounds, so too, in a work of literature, the theme is an implicit or recurrent background perspective on life. One could say that, generally, it is the author's own perspective which is disclosed by means of the characters and plot. Readers need not necessarily agree with the author's implied views. Nevertheless, coming up against ideas that differ from our own forces us to re-think, re-evaluate what we believe about human experience. Theme in good literature is subtle because it arises out of the interplay of the work's parts; perhaps it is hinted at in the thoughts or statements of various characters, or by the way conflicts are resolved, etc.

One theme of *Secret of Lost Mountain* is that miracles do happen and that miraculous happenings can give rise to faith, just as it is true to say that faith can give rise to miracles. A second theme focuses on the wholesomeness of family relationships. A third theme touches on the dignity of people who are physically challenged.

QUESTIONS ABOUT THEME

A

- This novel deals with *miracles*, and with belief or unbelief in their possibility. How many miracles are mentioned or described in the story?

B

- Throughout the novel an undercurrent keeps reappearing—the desirability and value of family and *familial relationships*. Where do you find references to father/son relationships? To parent/child relationships? Does the author point out a difference between modern families and primitive families?

C

- We come away from the novel with a firm admiration for the *Jakareme* who, despite profound *physical challenges*, have formed a community of love and support. How does the author demonstrate the dignity of their lives?

RESPONSES AND OBSERVATIONS

A. Miracles in the Story

A theme about the power of God to work miracles steadily emerges as a series of inexplicable events associated with the saint's relic overcomes the explorer's agnosticism, causing him to wish for and then actually help effect the miraculous healing of Sweet Berry.

- The man of science is first (ironically) introduced to belief in miracles by the faith that the entire *Chiroki* community has in the power of the relic. This because of the miraculous healing of *Teeku-mi* as a small *Jakareme* child.

- The explorer is stunned to witness how the entire *Jakareme* community is being fed with two loaves of bread and a few fish.

- Sweet Berry's role in that feeding, and her immediate and spontaneous attraction to the relic might be seen as a kind of miracle in itself.

- The miraculous healing of Sweet Berry's blindness seems fully established when the native prince *Teeku-mi* prostrates himself before the explorer and the explorer sees the miracle in the native's glistening eyes.

- The transformation of the *Jakareme* [children of the curse] into *Odiliareme*, and therefore their re-integration with the *Chiroki* tribe, is a miracle.

- Of course, the many events, big and small, that led an unbelieving man of science to become the instrument of miraculous healing, almost against his will, can be seen as signs of miraculous leading. The novel certainly suggests as much.

- In the *Afterword*, we learn that, historically and even to this day, St. Odilia is revered for causing healings, particularly that of blindness.

B. Father/Son and Parent/Child relationships

The story of this novel is permeated with parent/child relationships. Fatherhood is a key theme in the novel.

- The youth with the broken arm was sitting in a shelter: *"There was an older native bending over him, like a father over an injured son."* (109)

- *"It was touching to see how keenly he [Teeku-mi] felt about family."* (76)

- *"Actually, he did have a son, but could say practically nothing about him. . . . The explorer reflected that he was somewhat of a disaster of a father, not like this aborigine. But that's how it was. Science had become his wife and child, perhaps by choice."* (77)

- The explorer works well with Charlie-two, repairing the thatched roofs. He realizes that he thinks of his own son in the past tense:

  o *"He has that same keenness my son had, or has I should say. (Why do I speak of him in the past tense?) It was gratifying how easily Charlie-two and I fell into a neat, relaxed work pattern."* (153)

- The explorer hopes to heal the relationship with his own son Charlie when he returns home:

  o *"He was more than ready to return to the coast and get back to his own people. Even see his son, Charlie, after these many years."* (192)

- There is no word in the *Jakareme* language for mothers and fathers. The explorer coins the word for father: "man mother."

- The *Jakareme* chief seems to have a "son" in the youngest of his underlings, Charlie-two:

- None of the *Jakareme* know what a mother or father is.

  o *"Little Sweet Berry is the only one here who knows her mother, who even knows what a mother is, the only one as far as I knew who ever remembers a mother's hand."* (179)

- The novel begins with the close relationship between Daisy, and her father who tells her a story about the deaf-blind. At the story's end we learn that Daisy herself is deaf-blind,

- The novel ends with a mother writing a poem about her deaf-blind daughter.

- In between are many parent/child relationships:
  o Carlito and his father.
  o *Teeku* is always spoken of as "son of *Maku.*" *Maku* in turn is son of *Timan* (as seen in a lineage chart).
  o *Matsitu* and his son *Teeku-mi.*
  o *Teeku-mi* and his daughter *Lunas nili* [Sweet Berry].
  o *Tolani* and her daughter *Lunas nili.*

- There's the original broken father/son relationship in the history of the *Chiroki* that started the *Jakareme* curse.

- The explorer briefly mentions his own medical doctor father, in whose steps he once considered following into medicine. And then of course, there is Father Damian, in whose steps the explorer unwittingly does follow throughout the story, virtually from beginning to end.

- The novel is a retelling of the relationship between Odilia and her father, a relationship that starts out with the father wanting to put Odilia away because of her blindness, even kill her, causing her to hide out in a cave. But in the end, she is miraculously healed and becomes reconciled to her father and cares for him at the time of his death. The author says the curious parallels here with the novel are entirely accidenttal. As he explains in the *Afterword*, the relic that figures so prominently in the novel did not take on the name Odilia until quite late in the story's composition, when the author, searching the Internet for a blind saint, discovered one that also, almost unbelievably, (1) was cast aside as a child by her father because of her blindness; (2) hid out in a cave; (3) was eventually cured of blindness and reconciled with her father. That coincidence in itself might seem like a miracle to some.

C. Dignity of the *Jakareme* People

The novel paints a picture of a certain richness in the lives of the *Jakareme* despite their poverty and their physical challenges.

- The novel depicts a community of people [the *Jakareme*] who do not and cannot live each man for himself. Their very survival depends on their having to look out for each other's welfare, each person quietly working for the common good, women providing meals and clothing, men foraging for food, fishing, and constructing living quarters. The story hints at the spiritual poverty of sighted people when they live only for themselves. In a way, the explorer himself starts out as an example of this.

- Rich relationships exist between many of the *Jakareme*, exemplified in the father-son relationships of Damian Two and Carlito-Two and also between the *Sabuknu* and his favorite staffer, Charlie Two.

- It would be well to consider what this need to depend on others does for human character. Notice there is no evidence of strife in the community. Notice how they care for each other and express concern for a lost member through communal action.

ALLEGORY OR LEVELS OF MEANING

Allegory is the representation of abstract ideas or principles by means of characters, figures, or events in narrative form (*American Heritage Dictionary*). Although we read an allegorical story as a narrative, in our reading we become aware of deeper *levels of meaning* that various characters, events and even things may represent.

QUESTIONS ABOUT ALLEGORY

A

- In what ways is the explorer a kind of *Christ figure*? Does the explorer do any of the things that Christ did as reported in the gospels?

B

- What is the deepest, *most fundamental Christ-like thing* the explorer did?

C

- Could *Secret of Lost Mountain* be considered a *salvation story*? What are some possible allegorical, Judeo-Christian elements in the novel?

RESPONSES AND COMMENTARY ABOUT ALLEGORY

A. Explorer as a Christ-like Figure

The explorer becomes a kind of "Christ figure" to the *Jakareme* in many ways, going about healing and performing good works.

- He puts additional fish into their reed baskets (like Jesus filling the nets of the apostles to the point of breaking).

- He carries the young boy out of the river and splints his broken arm.

- He finds the little lost boy who is splashing in the river and delivers him to his guardians, like the Good Shepherd seeking the lost sheep.

SECRET OF LOST MOUNTAIN

- He takes the splinter out of Sweet Berry's foot.

- He helps rebuild damaged dwellings.

- He heals *Tolani's* fever, thus saving her life.

- He saves the life of Charlie-two by killing the panther that was about to attack the *Jakareme* native.

- He feeds the "multitude" with two loaves and a few fish.

- He effects the restoration of sight to a blind girl.

B. Deeper Likeness to Christ

- Notice how the explorer only gradually begins to understand his mission. The message of the first priest *("Tell* Sabuknu *I offer my death for them.")* initially meant little to the explorer. But then, in the scene at the altar, he begins to grasp the greater significance of his role. *"The explorer, vested now in the priest's very own garments, caught a glimpse just then of what that message might have meant."* (73)

- Just as Christ died for the redemption of mankind, ultimately the explorer also dies, like the priest Christopher Damian, in order to redeem the accursed *Jakareme.*

C. Salvation Story and Allegorical Elements

- The view of the deaf-blind as "children of the curse" could be considered allegorical to the biblical story of Adam and Eve and their offspring as "children of the Fall." Adam and Eve rebelled against the will of their Creator and as a result are cast out from the Garden of Eden. All their progeny are "born blind" into a world in which God is only dimly remembered. *Chiroki* history too is marred by a great sin, and the *Jakareme* must pay for it. They become outcasts from their rightful home. Their plight on Lost Mountain is a symbol of the human condition before its redemption. We are reminded that Jesus came to save what was lost.

36

- In the novel, salvation is manifested in a number of ways: (1) by the *reconciliation* of broken family relationships, e.g.,*Tolani* and her husband *Teeku-mi;* (2) by the *restoration* of the *Jakareme* to their *Chiroki* kinsmen; (3) salvation is symbolically expressed in the restoration of sight to Sweet Berry; and, finally (4) salvation is announced when the *Jakareme*, children of the curse, are given a new *name, Odiliareme*, children of *Odilia.*

- Just as the human race needed an intercessor, so too do the *Jakareme* require an intermediary who will act as mediator on their behalf to transform their life. The explorer sees *"no reason for them [the* Jakareme*] to be kept apart like this, not one day longer."* (162)

  o The first priest, Christopher Damian, like an Old Testament prophet, identifies the problem and prepares the way.

  o The second "priest" accomplishes his mission in New Testament fashion by sacrificing his life.

- Ministering angels (like the *Jakareme* mothers) assist humans in tasks too difficult to carry out on their own.

- The intercessory role of Odilia is fundamental to almost everything good that happens in the book, just as is intercession fundamental to Christian salvation generally. Jesus *"intercedes for us at the right hand of the Father."*

- This story could easily be seen as an allegory of human life generally: imperfect humans make their way in an often unfriendly world without the advantage of true sight or hearing.

- More specifically, this aspect of the novel also can give rise to fruitful discussion about the plight of the disadvantaged in society and about diversity, those who are different from us, and finally about the lives of those who are physically challenged.

SYMBOLISM

The novel has a number of symbolic elements. The dictionary defines a symbol as "something that stands for or suggests something else by reason of relationship, association, convention, or accidental resemblance." For example, a lion is a symbol of courage, as in the expression "lion-hearted."

QUESTIONS ABOUT SYMBOLS IN THE NOVEL

A

Since this is a story about blindness, about attempts to bring light to people in darkness, what significance does the *flashlight* play in the novel?

A *ring* is a symbol of one's identification with another (as in a class or school ring); or of one's union with another (a wedding ring). What significance does the ring of *Teeku* play in the story?

B

Sometimes fictional characters are given *names* that signify something of their personality or their role in the novel. What symbolism do you find in the names Christopher and Sweet Berry?

C

In the story, the *relic* is the agent of healing, and of other key and highly improbable events also, but what does a relic really signify? Does the *color "purple"* (of the sashes used to identify the *Jakareme* mothers) signfy anything? What special meaning might the terms *"secret," "lost"* and *"mountain"* in the book's title signify?

RESPONSES AND COMMENTARY ABOUT SYMBOLISM

A. Symbolism of the *Flashlight* and the *Ring*

The flashlight functions as a key symbol of light in a novel that is full of images of light and darkness. Not everyone is "enlightened" in the same way. In fact, everyone in the novel is blind in some way:

- The explorer sees himself as a "son of the Enlightenment." The flashlight is a product of the "enlightened" modern world. The first incidence of the flashlight is its power to convert the war-like demeanor of the natives into mirth, natives who have never seen such a thing as artificial light. However, at the outset, the explorer himself is blind to the light of faith. He becomes en-lightened at the end, ironically by the intervention, in part, of people who are blind.

- The *Chiroki* are blind to the knowledge of modern medicine and the causes of physical infirmities. They live in the darkness of superstition and the curse that superstition has imposed on their afflicted members. In the end the entire *Chiroki* tribe is liberated from dread of Lost Mountain by a new kind of light, supernatural in origin.

- The flashlight is first presented to the *Chiroki* as a gift. It is re-jected as *Teeku-mi* dashes it on the ground at the explorer's feet. This act signifies *Chiroki* rejection of the explorer and everything he stands for, i.e., the enlightened world that he rep-resents. By contrast, in the last scenes of the novel, *Teeku-mi* is presented with the flashlight once again, and this time he ac-cepts it and enters the cave to discover the miracle. "Light" in many forms is beginning to transform him and through him the *Jakareme*, and eventually the entire *Chiroki* tribe.

- The flashlight is also the instrument that revealed to the explor-er the apparent miracle of Sweet Berry. This also marks the be-ginning of his own transformation, as he suddenly gains cour-age and confidence that his dreamed of miracle will actually take place: the elimination of the fear of Lost Mountain, and the restoration of the *Jakareme* to their people.

The ring is a symbol of union, of belonging. There are many ex-changes of rings throughout.

- As *Teeku* gives his ring to the explorer, he says, "*It family ring,*" adding, "*for men of family.*" (36)

- Through the gift of the ring, the explorer symbolically becomes a member of the *Chiroki* noble family (and eventually gives his life for them).

- The explorer gives his *Chiroki* family ring to the *Jakareme Sabuknu,* prefiguring the eventual re-uniting of the *Jakareme* (through their *Sabuknu*) with the *Chiroki,* which occurs at the story's end.

B. Symbolism in Names

Sweet Berry is an image—or symbol—of Odilia herself, as suggested by the immediate and spontaneous way the young girl takes to the relic.

- Sweet Berry becomes an agent of the reconciliation between her mother and father, as the historical St. Odilia was the agent of reconciliation between her father and her brother.

- Sweet Berry has many saintly qualities, particularly her sanguine nature which caused her to have such equilibrium, as seen, for example, in the way she responds to the explorer's sudden and unforeseen approach to her, or when the little boy was lost and everyone else but she and the explorer was upset. The explorer recognizes in her a love for the truth. Her compassion is apparent in her solicitude for her mother and for the children she taught.

- Her name itself is symbolic, expressing something about her moral character. Her disposition is unusually sweet and compliant and the word "berry" brings to mind sweet delights.

Fr. Christopher Damian – He is the real, prototype priest whose concern and sacrifice for the *Jakareme* the explorer, as pseudo priest, unwittingly imitates. In a dramatic scene near the story's end, the explorer in fact momentarily seems to become this priest, and from that point on finally completes the unfulfilled mission begun by Christopher Damian.

- The name "Christopher" literally means "Christ Bearer." Fr. Christopher Damian first brought Christ and the Christian faith to the *Chiroki.*

C. Symbolism of the *Relic*, the *Purple Color*, and of the Book's Title, *Secret of Lost Mountain*

The *relic* – Clearly, the relic of St. Odilia is the secret protagonist of the story virtually from the beginning, when the explorer unknowingly attributes his good fortune in finding *Teeku* to "lady luck."

- A relic is like the tip of an iceberg. Underneath it is the real power that God and God alone allows it to have, so in the final analysis a relic is just a sign and instrument of that power. As the novel says of the explorer, near the story's climax, *"But in that moment, outside himself, he believed in the priest Damian, and this priest believed in a miracle-working saint, and this saint believed in a God of miracles, a God who could do anything He wished. It's what makes a saint a saint and even an agnostic man of science had to acknowledge this."* (189)

The *purple color* – In the liturgy of the Church, purple is always symbolically a penitential color.

- The mothers of the *Jakareme* spend their lives in a penitential situation imposed on them by the community. The purple sashes they were obliged to wear signify that state.

The title, *Secret of Lost Mountain*

- Two *secrets* are involved in this story. One is the secret of the *Jakareme,* whether they in fact even exist, and, once that is established, why they have been banished to Lost Mountain and how they ever managed to survive on their own. A second secret pertains to the hidden power of the relic which seems to account for the explorer's compulsion to find the *Jakareme,* to say nothing of subsequent events after he does find them. Both secrets are only gradually revealed as the story develops.

- The combination of the terms "*lost*" and "*mountain*" would seem to be almost contradictory, since mountains can hardly be lost. Valleys might be lost because of being hidden, but mountains are among the most visible things imaginable.

- The mountain's association with the term "lost," then, has to do with the circumstances associated with it: that it is the home of fearsome, evil spirits, and because of that is off-limits to the

Chiroki. And it is the place to which the deaf-blind members of the *Chiroki* tribe are banished, so that the *Jakareme* and the *Chiroki* become *lost* to each other. The mountain, though it is "lost to sight" as far as the *Jakareme* are concerned, is nevertheless good to them in its abundance of fish, vegetables, fruits and nuts which keep them alive.

OTHER ASPECTS: LANGUAGE

This novel raises some interesting questions about the role of language in our lives.

QUESTIONS ABOUT LANGUAGE

A

How many languages (of various kinds) have been mentioned in the novel?

B

On the final page of the novel, a poem speaks about *"a common language."* What is the "common language" in *Secret of Lost Mountain*? Is language ever more than words? For example, could the language of touch be just as rich as verbal language? In this regard, how did the *Jakareme* communicate affection and friendship?

C

In the last pages of Chapter 12, the explorer's reflection about language raises an interesting question about *the way language affects our thinking.* For example, what comes first, a thing or the word for that thing? An idea or feeling, or the word for that idea or feeling? Can we have one without the other? How do we think words get created?. Answers to such questions may even border on the philosophical notion that language shapes our culture and our perception of reality as much as the other way around.

A, B, C

A question for all. Did the author's discussion about language, and his inclusion in the novel of so many kinds of language, increase your interest in and appreciation of foreign languages? Did it teach you something about language you hadn't considered before?

RESPONSES AND OBSERVATIONS ABOUT LANGUAGE

A. Languages

Seven languages of various kinds are involved in the story.

SECRET OF LOST MOUNTAIN

- The first, of course, is the explorer's own, **native language,** i.e., the language in which the story is being told.

- The second is the **Latin** used by the Jesuit priest to speak of the rumors regarding a mysteriously silent people. This Latin note caught the explorer's attention and triggered his adventure.

- When the explorer arrives at the coastland he communicates in **Moulawi,** the local language that he'd come to master in preparation for this adventure.

- The explorer hears Carlito and his father speak a **patois** or dialect variation of *Moulawi,* which the explorer isn't able to follow.

- A list of words in the **Chiroki** language is found in the envelope belonging to Carlito's father. From *Teeku* the explorer learns how to use these words to make simple *Chiroki* sentences. He studies and memorizes what he learned as he makes his way up the river, making it possible for him to communicate with the *Chiroki* tribe, although in a most limited way.

- *Teeku* also taught the explorer some significant **signs and gestures,** which in themselves constitute a kind of unspoken language. The explorer communicated his disposition through the signs in confrontations on the river, and then later among the *Chiroki,* almost always to good effect.

- The explorer exploits the **language of "trinkets"** that he knows will "speak" to the various local tribes as he canoes up the river, "a language all would understand."

- The explorer learns and uses rudiments of their **palming language** to communicate with the *Jakareme.*

- **Knot codes** on the identity strings worn by the *Jakareme.* Similar codes are also used to identify trails on vine lines.

B. The "Common Language"

- Once the explorer meets the *Jakareme,* verbal communication is impossible and must take the form of actions, such as drawing symbols on hands, feeling for identity strings, dressing wounds, feeding, and, ultimately, dying.

- Communication in this novel takes many forms therefore. But in the end, we may understand that the ultimate "common language" is simply the communication of our presence to each other. This is expressed by the real-life, deaf-blind girl in the poem appearing at the novel's end. The poem was written on her behalf by her sighted mother. Entitled "A Common Language," the poem tells us this is the language of love, of being there for another. The poems ends with the poignant question, "Are you there?" In effect, the poem reveals that the language of love is beyond words and is common to all.

C. The Language Effect

Each reader will have a different response to the question of how language affects our thinking.

- Consider the author's suggestion that the language conceived by the *Jakareme*, while deficient in many terms such as "sky" and "thunder" and "music," nevertheless could very well be rich in other concepts dealing with human relations, human need and human affection. The explorer himself ponders this: *"I can well believe that they exchange words among themselves that my language is poor in. Why wouldn't that be so? There's no shortage here of intelligence, of feeling, of desire, of want."* (144)

- The explorer also ponders the irony that none of the *Jakareme* understands such notions as mother, father, brother, sister, or spouse; none of them having any experience of these realities. But they understand very well the notion of friend and have hand signs for affection, gratitude and so on.

- Some instructors may want to bring in discussion here about the monastic tradition of contemplative monks (both Western and Eastern traditions) who limit the use of spoken language in preference for silence. Students might research this tradition, e.g., among the Trappists, which relies on sign language more than on spoken words.

A NOTE ABOUT THE AUTHOR'S "AFTERWORD"

The last-page disclosure of Odilia as a real, historical saint could raise questions about the actuality of other aspects of the story. Has anything remotely like this ever really happened? Not likely, but the aura of actuality that hovers over the story might seem strengthened by this final, stunning disclosure of an actual blind saint who, because of her blindness, was cast out by her father; who also hid out in a cave; whose sight was miraculously restored; and who was eventually reconciled with her father.

The author, Bernard Scott, has said that Odilia had nothing to do with the origin of this story as far as he was concerned. He did not even know of her existence when he began. And that, well into the story, he still had no clear idea how the tale would end. As he was writing he always felt that Sweet Berry and her father would have to be reconciled, but that the curing of her blindness was beyond the scope of the novel. As he got near the end, however, he felt he had no choice in the matter, as if her cure simply had to happen.

Authors say they are often amazed at the choices and behavior of their characters when the authors allow them to play out their own inclinations. This is especially true in the case of this novel. The author says that he often felt the story was being "given" to him as he went about the writing. But that's not unusual. Every writer experiences inspiration, and when it happens, no one can be sure where the inspiration came from. So who knows, the author seems to be suggesting in his "Afterword," maybe St. Odilia herself had something to do with this story and the rather mysterious way it unfolds.

ADVANCED RESEARCH

The Deaf-Blind

There are thousands of deaf-blind people in the United States who function in the world with admirable facility. The author of *Secret of Lost Mountain* first conceived of the novel's plot when he read the life of Helen Keller and learned how she achieved such success in life as an author. Research on the topic of the deaf-blind may "open our eyes" to a new understanding of the human spirit. The internet is a special boon to the deaf-blind because, with Braille terminals, they are able to communicate effectively with the world.

Suggested websites:

> **http://www.aadb.org**
>
> **http://www.deafblind.com**
>
> **http://www.HKI.org**

Relics

Relics, their variety, their role in religion, and their place and effects in history might make an interesting subject for research.

Suggested website:

> **http://www.newadvent.org/cathen/12734a.htm**

St. Odilia

Research this saint and the miracles she has worked over the centuries.

Suggested websites:

> **http://en.wikipedia.org/wiki/Odile_of_Alsace**
>
> **http://en.wikipedia.org/wiki/Odilia_of_Cologne**

ABOUT THE AUTHOR

Arlene Scott is a Professor of English who is now retired from a lifetime of teaching literature and writing. She received her M. A. in English Language and Literature from the University of Michigan. Her teaching career ranged from junior high school through high school, where she became chair of the English department. She ended her teaching career as Assistant Professor of English at Sussex County Community College in northern New Jersey where she became a recipient of the NISOD award for teaching and leadership excellence.

www.ingramcontent.com/pod-product-compliance
Lightning Source LLC
Chambersburg PA
CBHW071216130626
46555CB00004B/1735